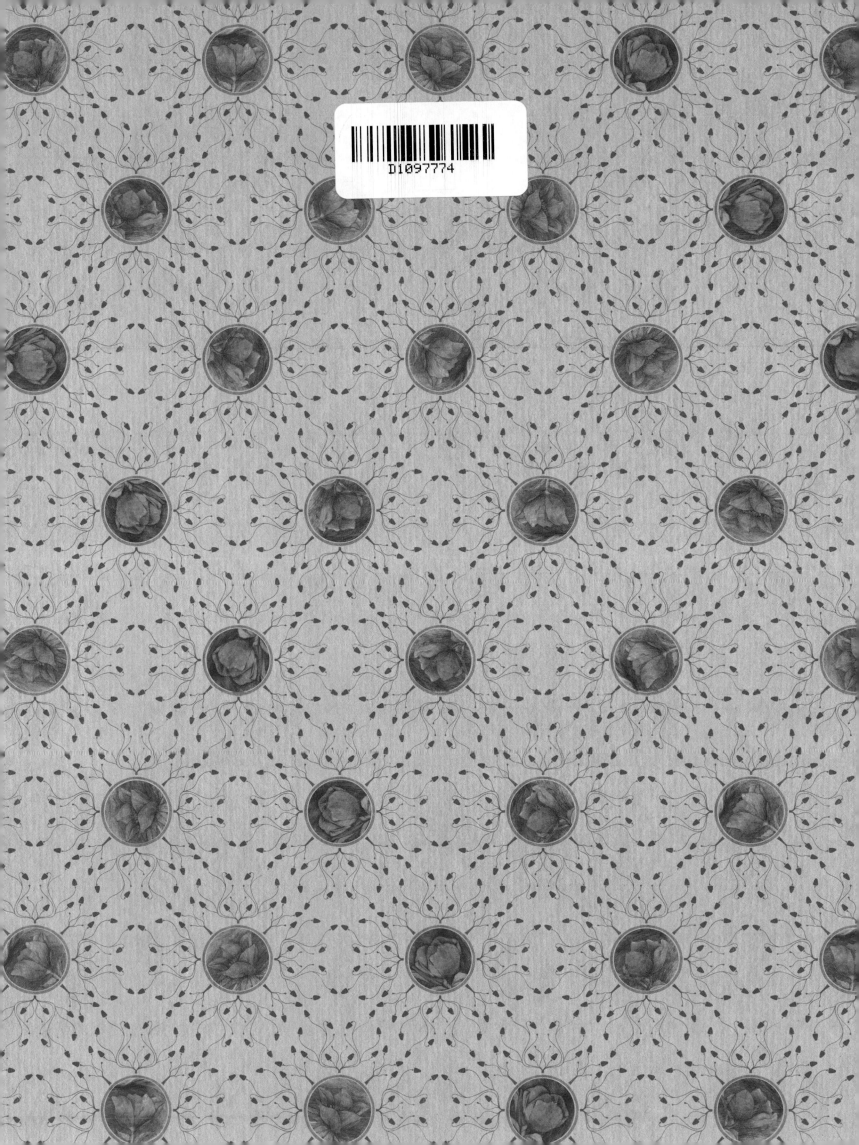

THE
FOREVER
FLOWERS

Text copyright © 2014 Michael J. Rosen   Illustrations copyright © 2014 Sonja Danowski
Designed by Rita Marshall   Edited by Kate Riggs
Published in 2014 by Creative Editions   P.O. Box 227, Mankato, MN 56002 USA
Creative Editions is an imprint of The Creative Company
Library of Congress Cataloging-in-Publication Data   Rosen, Michael J.
The forever flowers / by Michael J. Rosen; illustrated by Sonja Danowski. Summary: A
young grouse packs a precious cargo of seeds for her migratory journey, only to find an
unexpected home in another land while she awaits the coming of another spring.
ISBN 978-1-56846-273-8   [1. Grouse—Fiction. 2. Seeds—Fiction.
3. Seasons—Fiction. 4. Birds—Migration—Fiction.] I. Danowski, Sonja, illustrator. II. Title.
PZ7.R71868Kee 2014   [E]—dc23   2013047407

First Edition 9 8 7 6 5 4 3 2 1

THE
FOREVER
FLOWERS

MICHAEL J. ROSEN

SONJA DANOWSKI

CREATIVE EDITIONS

EPIGRAPH

Summer begs autumn to brag of its abundance. Oh, autumn tries. It fills the land with sun-drenched colors. But patient winter insists on white, all white, so spring can ask its same green question: *What next, old world?*

Even as autumn's days shortened and chilled, and even as frosted trees shrugged off their colors, a rose-cheeked grouse clung to summer. Her favorite Forever Flowers—the first to appear, the last to disappear—barely poked above the sudden snowfall.

"It's time to go!" her older friends pleaded. "Another spring awaits us."

"It's time I need! More time!" the young grouse replied. She stuffed a grass packet she'd woven with seeds. She plucked the last Forever Flower.

"Leave all that," one friend advised.

"Hang on to what's old, and you miss something new," the other added.

But she didn't listen.

Like three plump clouds, the grouses soared into a sky so gray the very air looked to be migrating to a land where colors yet bloomed.

The older grouses glided higher, but the younger bird struggled to stay aloft. Her packet grew heavier. Winds plucked petals from her flower.

Over a great river, the grouse sank lower and lower until her wings—hopelessly heavy—thrashed the air one last time to soften her plunge into autumn's icy water.

Nearby, in a world that only seemed far-away, a springer spaniel witnessed the splash of the gray cloud. He sprinted across the field—no thought of returning the ball some-one had been tossing—leapt into the water, and paddled alongside the exhausted bird.

The grouse scrambled onto the spaniel's back. His lips lifted into a smile around the ball. He could see that she, too, carried some-thing she didn't want to let go.

The dog followed the shoreline until it bent closest to the cottage he knew as home.

Alongside the muffled drum of the dog's heart and the calm drafts of his breaths, the grouse fell asleep. A soft snoring reverberated from the next room. The chimney's smoke plumed. Tiny wafts of air escaped the grouse's beak. Not quite in rhythm, the whole cottage breathed together.

The dog's warmth tucked among her feathers, the sleepy grouse joined her rescuer and his companion. Each stared into the vacant gray; only the grouse longed for something more than the sun to rise.

Finally, the spaniel broke away, returning with the grouse's packet. He could have told the bird, "Stay. Spring will come before you know it." Instead, he set her packet beside his companion's hand, and she peered inside.

Even before daybreak, the potted seeds began to awaken.

Darkness buried some days. Sunlight lifted others. The grouse, it appeared, felt that impatience could hurry the seasons. But the spaniel showed her that the way to pass time is to revel in it: romp through snow, sniff trails, fetch.

Yet the grouse thought only of leaving and the happiness she'd left behind. She counted the new petals on her Forever Flower seedlings as if each one brought her closer to spring and back to her friends.

After three unexpectedly warm days, the snow disappeared.

The spaniel assured her the wait was hardly over: The grouse's seedlings—still tiny—provided proof.

But even the dog's companion seemed restless. With lunch bundled into a basket, the three walked along the river and picnicked close to where, months ago, the grouse had been rescued.

In the language all creatures share, the spaniel and his companion could tell that the grouse wanted this almost-spring day to stay and stay until the season truly arrived. But they didn't know how to convince her that happiness comes from the very chance of stumbling upon it again.

A darkening chill ushered the three home. There, the grouse snuggled into the curve of the spaniel's body. As he drifted to sleep, his sigh persuaded the bird to let her perfect day set contentedly like the sun.

How many such moments passed that winter? The grouse couldn't say. But she had seen her seedlings reach higher: two … four … six paired leaves. She'd watched their buds arise: timidly bowed … cautiously lifted … and, now, dizzily offering their petals—the very color of her cheeks—to the sunlight. The Forever Flowers were now large enough to plant.

Just as gradually, the bird had grown into the life of the cottage. All three creatures had found a space for each other in their full hearts.

Although snow continued to argue for winter, the sun had climbed higher in the sky. Spring neared, and the three prepared for the season as if it were the guest of honor. They planted the grouse's flowers. They draped lanterns around the cottage. And the party guests? Their companion fashioned them from snow.

Nearby, in a world that only seemed faraway, the grouse's friends spied the lanterns' rosy glow and dove toward the river where they'd lost their friend.

"We knew it had to be you!" one friend exclaimed.

"And you have the very first of the earliest Forever Flowers!"

Happiness outshined all the lanterns. The young grouse asked them to stay.

"How can we?" her friends replied. "Spring awaits us—and you."

The spaniel and his companion didn't need to answer the question their new friend was too sad to ask: *Of course, you'll miss us. Of course, you'll be missed.*

The grouse did not know what to do. Stay or fly away? Keep these first days of spring as she had tried to hold on to the last of summer, or let go?

 As the sun rose on the first day of spring, the dog and his companion watched three gray clouds lift into the entirely blue sky. Two soared higher and higher. One, as if forgetting—or, maybe, remembering—something, soared down toward the great river where a dog once chased a ball someone was tossing.